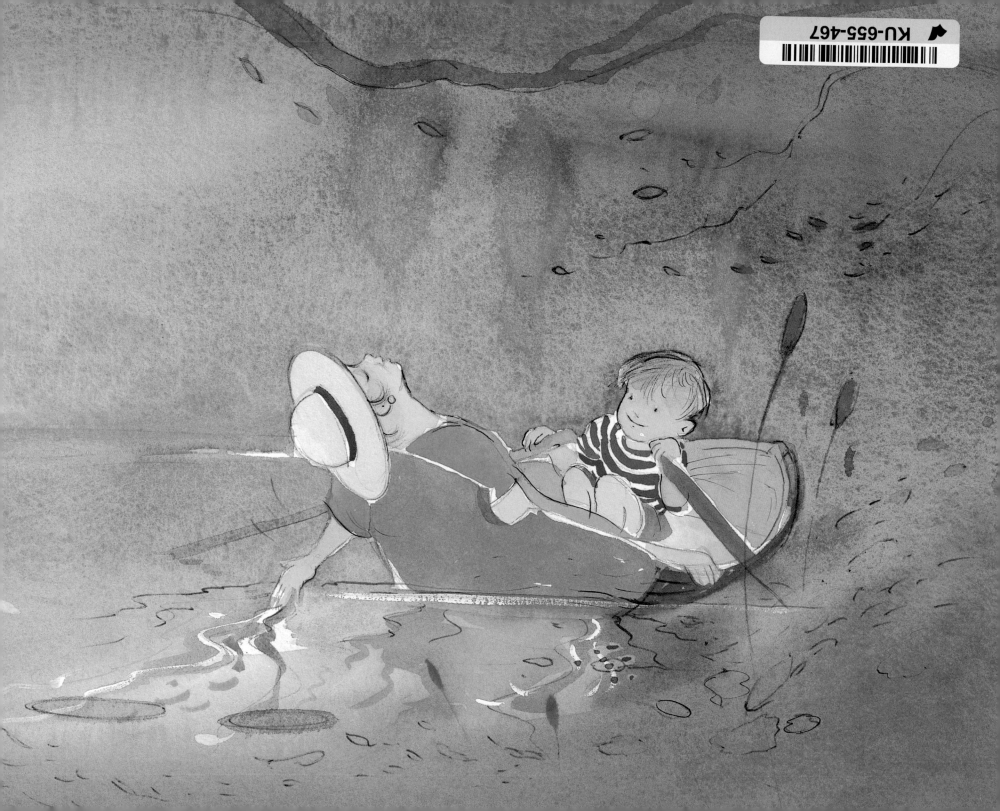

Row  Boat

Lisa Bruce • Robin Bell Corfield

Row, row, row your boat
Gently down the stream.
Merrily, merrily, merrily, merrily,
Life is but a dream.

Row, row, row your boat
Quickly up the river.
When the wind blows very hard,
We'll begin to shiver.

Row, row, row your boat
On the silvery lake.
If a wave comes rolling by,
Our little boat will shake.

Row, row, row your boat
Swiftly out to sea.
Can you see the pretty fish
Swim from you to me?

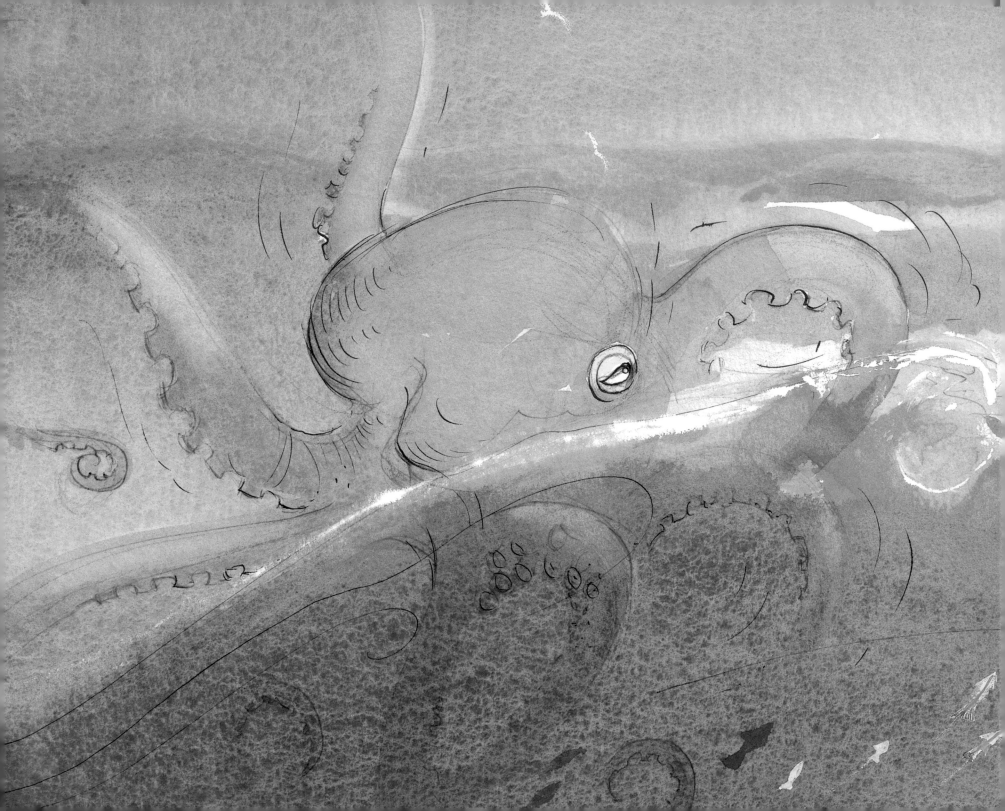

Row, row, row your boat
Across the ocean wide.
See the eight-legged octopus
Swim away and hide.

Row, row, row your boat
Slowly up the stream.
If you see a crocodile,
Don't forget to scream.

Row, row, row your boat
Home on the lagoon.
If you look up to the sky,
You will see the moon.

Row, row, row your boat
Sitting on the floor.
Are you getting tired now,
Or shall we sing once more?

Act Out the Rhyme!

Row, row, row your boat
Gently down the stream.
Merrily, merrily, merrily, merrily,
Life is but a dream.

Row, row, row your boat
Quickly up the river.
When the wind blows very hard,
We'll begin to shiver.

Row, row, row your boat
On the silvery lake.
If a wave comes rolling by,
Our little boat will shake.

Row, row, row your boat
Swiftly out to sea.
Can you see the pretty fish
Swim from you to me?

Row, row, row your boat
Across the ocean wide.
See the eight-legged octopus
Swim away and hide.

Row, row, row your boat
Slowly up the stream.
If you see a crocodile,
Don't forget to scream.

Row, row, row your boat
Home on the lagoon.
If you look up to the sky,
You will see the moon.

Row, row, row your boat
Sitting on the floor.
Are you getting tired now,
Or shall we sing once more?

Music for the Rhyme

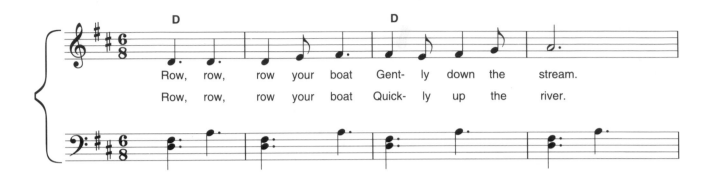

Row, row, row your boat Gent- ly down the stream.
Row, row, row your boat Quick- ly up the river.

Mer- ri- ly, mer- ri- ly, mer- ri- ly, mer- ri- ly, Life is but a dream.
When the wind blows ve- ry hard, We'll be gin to shiver.

Row Your Boat copyright © Frances Lincoln Limited 2001
Text copyright © Lisa Bruce 2001. Illustrations copyright © Robin Bell Corfield 2001
Music arranged by Margaret Lion

First published in Great Britain in 2001 by Frances Lincoln Limited,
4 Torriano Mews, Torriano Avenue, London NW5 2RZ

ISBN 0-7112-1557-X hardback

Printed in Hong Kong

1 3 5 7 9 8 6 4 2